The Village of Round and Square Houses

Ann Grifalconi

Little, Brown and Company
Boston □ New York □ Toronto □ London

*This village really exists—just the way it always has—
in the remote hills of the Cameroons in Central Africa.
It is almost entirely isolated, with no paved roads closer
to it than a full eight hours away. None but the most
adventurous visitor would dare risk the steep and bumpy,
rocky clay paths leading to the thatch-roofed village
that clings to the side of an almost extinct volcano.
Today, the village of Tos remains—
I know, for I have been there….
The homesick girl who brought us there told us its story.*

—A. G.

10 9 8 7 6 5 4 3 2 1

Library of Congress Cataloging-in-Publication Data
Grifalconi, Ann.
     The village of round and square houses.

     Summary: A grandmother explains to her listeners why in their village on the side of a volcano the men live in square houses and the women in round ones.
     [1. Folklore—Cameroon]   I. Title.
PZ8.1.G874Vi   1986   398.2'7'096711   [E]   85-24150
ISBN 0-316-32859-6

BP
*Published simultaneously in Canada
by Little, Brown & Company (Canada) Limited*

Printed in the United States of America

It was not until I was almost full-grown and left my village

That I found our village was like no other.

For the men live in SQUARE houses, and the women, in ROUND ones!

To me, this seemed the natural order of things....

"But what is it like?" you ask.

I will tell you how it was—and is—for me.

I grew up on my grandmother's farm in the village of Tos

That lies at the foot of Naka Mountain in the Bameni Hills of west Africa.

We planted yams and corn and tobacco

And the finest coffee grown in the Cameroons.

Our village was always happy and peaceful—

A good place for any boy or girl to grow up.

Every evening, after a day of work in the fields—
Uncle Domo and Gran'pa Oma came to our round house for supper.
We children would hurry to put out the low, wooden stool for Gran'pa Oma
(For he was the eldest, and closer to the ancestor spirits).
Then we would unroll the grass mat for Uncle Domo, the next oldest,
As was only proper and respectful.

And there they would sit proudly in their bright robes—
Gran'pa Oma above, seated on his stool, hands on knees—
And Uncle Domo seated below.
Then they would ask to see the children!
One by one we would come forward from the narrow doorway…
And one by one, we would be lifted to sit upon those high and bony knees,
And Gran'pa would ask each one of us, "What have you learned today?"

We would squirm and make an answer

And wriggle off those sharp knees

And run to help Mama and Gran'ma Tika prepare the meal to come.

Supper might be fish or rabbit or ground-nut stew or yams—

But always *I* would be the one to pound and soften the white cassava root,
To make the *fou-fou* we eat at every meal.
Then Mama would cook the *fou-fou* and beat it 'til it was white and fluffy
And she would pile the food into big bowls with round handles—
Just right for our small hands to hold.

Then we would march into the big round room—
Our bare feet gripping the earthen floor.
The little ones went first, carrying the bowl of heated water and towels
To wash the hands before and after eating.
Then the older ones would carry in the stew,
Spicy and steaming—smelling oh, so good!
And I would come in last bearing the *fou-fou!*

Gran'pa, as the eldest, would always eat first,
Dipping the first three fingers of one hand into the *fou-fou*—
Scooping up a small portion which he dipped *quickly* into the stew bowl,
To flavor each bite with the spicy meat and juices!
Then, in order of age—Gran'ma, Uncle Domo, and sometimes Mama
(If she left the cook fire) would finish their meal in the same way,
And we children would follow last—making sure to leave the bowl clean!

After supper, when the men went back to their square house

To smoke, and talk of farming and fishing and the old days of the hunt,

Gran'pa would leave some tobacco for Gran'ma.

(He knew she liked to smoke it later—when everything was peaceful.)

Then she would sit alone in the moonlight, looking up at the dark slope

Of Naka Mountain, rising high above....

I remember one night I sat beside her—Gran'ma Tika took a last puff on her pipe
Then pointed with it to the sky above our village.
"You see old Mother Naka smoking so peacefully there?"
I leaned way back and looked up to see old Naka's breath
Rising in lazy puffs of smoke, soft and gray in the night sky.

"And you remember that sometimes in the night
We hear old Naka snoring in her sleep?"
I nodded, pleased that Gran'ma felt I was old enough to notice such things.
"Well, it is by these signs that we know she is content.
Now, we live in peace with Naka and the spirits of our ancestors,
But it was not always so!"

Gran'ma fixed me with a stare

And began to rock with the tale...

For she was the best storyteller in the whole village!

"In the days of long, long ago,
The people of this village lived
In houses of any sort, either square or round,
It did not matter.

"Then, one peaceful night
Before anyone alive remembers
Old Naka began to groan and rumble
And awoke from a long sleep!

"The villagers were frightened
And ran out of their houses
And hid in the bushes
At the foot of the mountain.

"A great wind came up
And the ancestor spirits in the trees
Cried out to warn them—
Even the rocks began to tremble!

"Suddenly, the black night
Was split open like a coconut!
And a great white burst of light
Rose like the sun!

"Then the voice of our mother Naka
Thundered out over all:
BOOM! BA-BOOM! BA-BOOM!

"And the people cried out to Naka,
And prayed where they were lying down,
Hands pressing the earth, asking:
'What have we done to so anger you?'

"All through the night
Old Naka spoke to them
Shouting her anger to the skies
As red rivers of lava flowed down her sides.

"The morning sun rose
But no one could see him—
The anger of Naka was too great
And ashes and smoke filled the air.

"Finally—
No one remembers when—
Naka spoke no more....

"Slowly—carefully—
The people lifted their heads and looked about:
Everything was covered with ashes—
Even themselves!

"Everyone looked like a gray ghost—
No one knew who stood next to them
Or who came behind....

"So they stood there—
Trembling with fear—
But grateful to be alive:
NAKA HAD SPARED THEM!

"Still covered with ashes—
The men, women, and children
Faced the mountain together
And went back to claim their homes.

"But when they came to the burned-out village,
Only two houses were left standing:
One SQUARE—   And one ROUND!

"The people saw that only
These two houses had been spared by Naka
And they wondered to themselves:
'*Why these?* Was it a sign?'

"But the village chief had no time
For such questions—
And he called them together:
'We must begin to rebuild our village now!'

"He pointed to the ash-covered people:
'You! TALL GRAY THINGS!
You go live in the SQUARE house!'

"'And you! ROUND GRAY THINGS—
Go live in the ROUND house!'

"'And you! SMALL GRAY THINGS over there!
You go pick the small gray stones out of the fields
So we can plant our crops again!'

"And so it was done.
The women lived in the round house with the children
And the women talked and laughed—
Preparing food for everyone.

"The men stayed in the square house
    And told each other tall stories
        And planted yams and corn
    Each day, in the new, rich soil.

"And the children made a game
Out of clearing the fields of small, gray stones
And went swimming and fishing in the long afternoons...

"And no one forgot to thank Naka
For sparing their lives
And giving them back such fine crops
From her good earth."

Gran'ma smiled down at me: "And so you see it has been to this day!

For the women have decided they *enjoy* getting together

To talk and to laugh and to sing

And the men have become *used* to being together,

And relaxing in their own place.

"And the children? Osa—is it not true
The children still keep the fields clear of little gray stones?"
"Yes!" I laughed. "And we still swim and play in the afternoon—
But we bring home the fish we catch for supper,
And we all get together then!"

Gran'ma laughed too: "So you see, Osa, we live together peacefully here—
Because each one has a place to be apart, and a time to be together...."
She took me by the hand and turned back to the round house.
"And that is how our way came about and will continue—

"'Til Naka speaks again!"